The DANGEROUS WORLD
of
JOE
MCGINTY

Written by Andy Mulligan • Illustrated by Lyn Knott

Published by Pearson Education Limited, Edinburgh Gate, Harlow, Essex, CM20 2JE
Registered company number: 872828

www.pearsonschools.co.uk

Text © Andy Mulligan 2011

Designed by Bigtop
Original illustrations © Pearson Education 2011
Illustrated by Lyn Knott

The right of Andy Mulligan to be identified as author of this work has been asserted by
him in accordance with the Copyright, Designs and Patents Act 1988.

First published 2011

15 14 13 12
10 9 8 7 6 5 4 3 2

British Library Cataloguing in Publication Data
A catalogue record for this book is available from the British Library

ISBN 978 1 408 27384 5

Printed and bound in Malaysia, (CTP-PPSB)

Acknowledgements
We would like to thank the children and teachers of Bangor Central Integrated Primary
School, NI; Bishop Henderson C of E Primary School, Somerset; Brookside Community
Primary School, Somerset; Cheddington Combined School, Buckinghamshire; Cofton
Primary School, Birmingham; Dair House Independent School, Buckinghamshire;
Deal Parochial School, Kent; Newbold Riverside Primary School, Rugby and Windmill
Primary School, Oxford for their invaluable help in the development and trialling of the
Bug Club resources.

Every effort has been made to contact copyright holders of material reproduced in this
book. Any omissions will be rectified in subsequent printings if notice is given to the
publishers.

CONTENTS

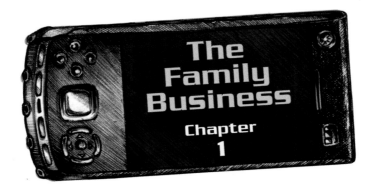

The Family Business

Chapter 1

Joe McGinty was settling down in his classroom to a morning of Maths.

This was a subject he particularly enjoyed, but then he enjoyed most subjects. If he had to pick three favourites they'd be Maths, judo and Japanese. He tried hard in all of them because his grandmother – whom he'd lived with for most of his life – told him that if he worked hard, he'd have a bright future in 'the family business'.

What that business was he'd never been able to discover, but he was content to keep the rules and do his best, in the hope that one day he'd find out.

It was quite a surprise then, when on this particular Thursday morning the headmaster appeared, looking even more irritable than usual, and called his name. When they got to the headmaster's office, Joe found three men in suits waiting for him.

The first was built like a bodyguard, and the second was as thin as a stick. The third tilted his bald head to one side and was smiling.

"These gentlemen want a word," said the headmaster. "It seems I have little choice in the matter, so here you are. I hope it won't take long."

"Oh," said Joe.

The man to the left was as big as a bear. He sniffed and said, "Scare easily, do you, Joe-boy?"

"Well ... not so far, sir."

The man raised his eyebrows. "Good answer."

"How many fire extinguishers did you pass as you came up the corridor?" asked the second man, quietly. His fingers rolled a long pencil.

"Three."

He ticked a sheet. "Hmm. Is that usual?"

"Um ... no, actually, sir. There are usually two, but a new one's appeared outside the boys' toilets. It used to be in the woodwork room."

"Very good. Any strangers in the building today that you're aware of?"

"Apart from you – let me think ... I saw a parent I didn't recognize in the library."

"She was a parent?"

"It was a he, actually, sir. Wearing a blue ID badge, which as far as I know, is only issued to parents. Is this some kind of test?"

"Yes," said the bald man, smiling more broadly. "Describe this parent to us, Joe."

The image flashed into Joe's mind:

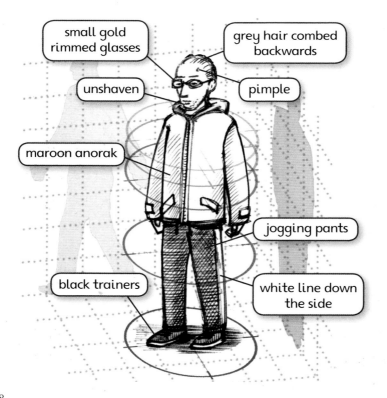

"Um … I'd say roughly the same age as our headmaster. He was wearing … a maroon anorak and jogging pants, white line down the side, and black trainers. Unshaven, and small gold rimmed glasses – a pimple on the forehead and thin grey hair that was combed backwards. I only saw him for a moment because he moved off down the fiction section, E to G."

"Joseph, my friend," said the big man. "Sit yourself down, please."

Joe sat.

"I think we'd better introduce ourselves. We work for the Government."

"You've come to our attention," said the thin man, "because for a 12-year-old boy you have a very special combination of skills. Those skills include mathematical excellence, and a power of observation and recall that puts you in the top 0.2 per cent of the country. Your motor skills are good, and your reflexes … "

He threw a tennis ball hard at the boy, and Joe caught it one-handed.

"… are exceptional. You don't scare easily, or so you claim. That, of course, we will put to the test in due course."

"Would you like to join us, and put your skills to the service of your country?" said the bald man.

"Yes," said Joe. "I think I would."

The headmaster turned from the window. Joe could see he was furious. "I thought that's what you'd say, McGinty, and I absolutely disapprove. I've been told to release you from school for one day a week and I have agreed, under protest. This kind of … melodramatic nonsense is clearly going to disrupt your education. I will grant you leave of absence on Thursdays only, and I expect you back on Friday morning – sharp. As far as teachers and children are concerned, this will be on the grounds of a serious illness."

"That's so you won't get asked awkward questions," said the thin man.

"Your training will be in-the-field and on the job," said the bear. "That's how we do things. We don't sit around in dull classrooms wasting the daylight. You'll be part of a small, select network."

"Your codename," said the bald man, "will be Lizard Seven."

"We won't be your handlers, Joe," said the thin one. "Nor can we guarantee your safety."

"You know I live with my gran?" said Joe. "I really think I ought to talk to her."

"Why is that?" said the bald man. He scratched his chin, thoughtfully.

"I'm not sure she'd approve of me missing school. We have a family business, you see … "

"Joe," said the bear. "This is the family business."

"What?"

"Trust your gran, do you?"

"With my life."

"Good answer."

The bald man's chin was getting puffier as he rubbed it, and his smile looked a little lopsided. In the silence that followed, he hooked his thumb into the crease that had opened, and started to peel his skin upwards.

His entire face was soon rolling towards his forehead, and his bald scalp then slipped to the side.

He removed a set of false teeth, and patted a rather flattened set of grey curls. Joe found that he was looking at the very grandmother he'd just spoken of.

His mouth opened, and he gasped.

"You're taking these shocks remarkably well, dear," she said.

"His heart rate's up," said the thin man, checking a curiously flat cellphone. "Gone up 18 per cent, which isn't bad."

"I wouldn't mind a glass of water," said Joe.

"No time, I'm afraid," said the bear. "A job's come up, and today is Thursday."

"Spying has always been in our family," said Joe's grandmother softly. "We're careful who we trust, and your dear parents were two of the finest agents we ever had. It was their dying wish that you'd follow in their footsteps. That, Joe, is the family business. Welcome to it."

"I think … " Joe paused. "I know you'd never put me in danger, Gran, but if – "

"Yes I would," she interrupted.

"Would you?"

"I don't have a choice."

"We live in a dangerous world," said the thin man. He pressed the pads on the cellphone and an alarm bell rang, faintly. "Our organization makes it safer, but to do that, we go into some heavy situations. This device is what we call a 'cellpad', issued to all our agents. It's going to be your lifeline. It's a coded Micra-2D7 which transmits and receives. It has a stun facility and a variety of tools you'll discover as you go. But you will be in danger, boy … and that's why my colleague asked you if you scared easily."

He opened a briefcase and withdrew a fat file of papers.

"We need your signature, of course," he said. "Once you've signed, there really is no going back."

"Life on Thursdays is about to change," said Joe's grandmother.

The cellpad rang.

"This will be Zeus," said the thin man. "Zeus is the ultimate boss, and the cellpad decodes her. Security is paramount, Joe – she only speaks through one of these. Now … "

He pressed a key, and a thin electronic voice emerged from the earpiece: "Is. He. Going. To. sign? Or not?"

Everyone looked at Joe.

"I think I will," he said.

"Good," said the thin man. "We needed you at the airport ten minutes ago."

Chapter 2

The airport was a small military base close to Joe's school. He was surprised to find himself waved through a number of security gates to the door of a twin-engined plane. He took a seat next to a very small girl. The pilot appeared from the cockpit, wearing his cap at a rakish angle.

"Pleased to meet you, Lizard Seven," he said. "I'm Ringo, and you'll be seeing a lot of me. I'm usually the Exit Man – channel 701 on your cellpad – a good man in a tight spot, so they say. Lizard Three will explain, no doubt.

This is Lizard Three, known for this mission as Tilly. On this little outing, she's your baby sister, so pull her hair as hard as you want to. Briefing docs are on your cellpad, so it's over to you. Get it all digested by 13:00 hours – Tilly will do a cross-check, and I'll fill in the gaps. Ooh – rolling already, are we?"

The plane was moving bumpily over the tarmac.

"I thought you were the pilot," said Joe.

"Well, I do the tricky bits," said Ringo. "Lizard Five's taking us up today – time he cut his teeth. Percival's his name for this mission and yours is Humphrey."

Joe peered into the cockpit and saw a tubby
boy with thick glasses at the controls. The boy
turned and raised his thumb, and the plane was
soon hurtling down the runway. As they rose
up into the clouds, Joe clicked his cellpad and
started reading.

"You're probably thinking I look rather young," said Tilly. "To be briefing you, I mean."

"No. I wasn't really thinking at all."

"I'm four. But I have a reading age of forty-three and an IQ of 207.

A toddler can get into all sorts of interesting places, as you'll see – they use me a lot. That's what's special about us Lizards. We can go where the grown-ups can't, so we move in after the Setters."

"Who are the Setters?"

"I'm forgetting how green you are." She spoke in a disconcertingly adult voice. "The Setters are the set-up people, who've been planning The Jump. The Jump, of course, is resolution."

"And that's … "

"Just before Exit – do you understand? The Setters have been following this particular team – we call them the Honey Men – for two and a half years, and we've had intelligence that they're shifting their honey tonight. The Lizards move in and hit them at the freight loader. Ringo does the Exit. You're extra cover and a receiver."

"Well … "

"Keep your ears and eyes wide open. You're a judo black belt?"

"Yes, but – "

"Restraint's often essential. We'll leave that up to you. Now I'd better take you through your cellpad."

"Wait … what's honey?"

"Sorry. Honey's what we call large denomination banknotes that have been forged, but are almost undetectable. They're spread around the world to destabilise the markets, and the villains cause chaos and rake up huge profits. One suitcase of honey can contain ten million dollars of totally fake money. The men we're following are the top dogs, pushing stuff to London. They're also carrying a laptop with the whole network on the hard-drive. Would you like a sweet?"

Tilly held out a lime-green lollipop.

"No, thank you."

"You ought to, really. It's good for cover. For example, I have to let my nose run and cry a lot. You have to behave exactly as a 12-year-old would behave, and that's how you get access. I have to carry this rabbit."

She took a pink rabbit from the seat beside her.

"It conceals my cellpad. You need to get changed, by the way. You have to look like one of those awful skater-boys."

Jo looked under his seat, and saw that a new costume awaited him. There was a huge faded T-shirt and a pair of baggy jeans. He hauled them all on. Bright trainers, a gold chain, and a baseball cap completed his transformation.

"You'd better chew some gum, as well," said Tilly. "Now go through the files and I'll test you in an hour."

Chapter 3

By the time Joe looked up again, they were flying through darkness.

Ringo, who'd been dozing behind them, leaned forward. "I'd better get back to the hot seat," he said. "Tricky bit coming up – smooth flight so far, wouldn't you say?"

"Yes," said Joe.

"I told them Lizard Five could do it, and done it he has. Things might get a bit bumpy, though – we have to drop fast and glide in under the radar. I'll be shutting the engines off, so don't panic. We almost have to touch down on the Istanbul bypass. We paid a traffic-cop for a two-minute window."

"I don't actually have a seat belt," said Joe, looking around him.

"Course you don't, you goof. You'll be through that door in five seconds, then I'm up again. What's your mission, Lizard Seven? Give me the bones."

"To be additional decoy for Lizard Three, sir."

"What's your role?"

"Obnoxious boy without self-control."

"What are we hoping?"

"That I'll receive the Honey Men's laptop and pass it to you, restraining suspects if necessary."

Ringo patted Joe on the shoulder. "Not bad at all," he said, grinning. "So good luck on your first sortie. I'd love to stay and chat, but the radar says I've a plane to fly."

Joe turned to Tilly.

He was about to ask a question when the plane dropped like a stone, and banked steeply to the right. He clung to his seat as they went into a near-vertical corkscrew, levelling and then accelerating so his cheeks were sucked together over his tongue. He put his hands over his ears at the scream of engines.

Suddenly, the engines simply cut out and the plane was coasting silently. Joe looked out of the window to see lamp posts and speeding trucks dangerously close.

Just when he thought they were all bound to die, a space opened in the traffic and the plane was hovering just above the road.

The engines burst back on in reverse thrust, and Joe saw Lizard Five heaving at the door controls.

A rush of cold air told him it was open, and then Tilly was pushing him through. The road zipped under them as – from nowhere – a tiny, open-topped sports car drew alongside, under the wing.

Remembering his judo, Joe jumped with his knees tucked in and found himself on the back seat of the car. He caught Tilly as she dropped after him. Percival arrived a split second later as the plane soared up and away into the darkness.

A blonde woman turned from the steering wheel and smiled. "Welcome to Istanbul, Lizards!" she said. "You've read your notes, but let's check the cover-story. We are a family, travelling first class to Bangkok for a skin-diving holiday. Daddy is waiting for us, and has obtained VIP clearance for the executive lounge. Beyond this remote and rarely used suite is FREIGHT LOADER 20, and the honey-drop takes place in … synchronize watches, please … forty-two minutes at midnight-zero-six. You have the rabbit, Lizard Three?"

"It's tied to my backpack, Mother," said Tilly.

Chapter 4

It didn't come easily to Joe to behave badly because his school was extremely strict.

However, the cellpad had instructed him, so as they approached the lounge he twisted his cap around and let his jeans slip towards his knees.

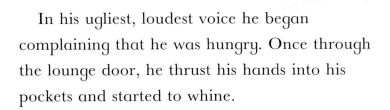

In his ugliest, loudest voice he began complaining that he was hungry. Once through the lounge door, he thrust his hands into his pockets and started to whine.

Tilly, meanwhile, tottered straight to a large window and started drawing on it with felt-tip pens. She sang loudly and tugged at her trousers. Percival had produced a skateboard from his bag and was immediately hurtling through the food displays, leaving piles of broken china behind him. They released a stink bomb each and argued at the tops of their voices.

The two other passengers stared in disbelief.

Mother, meanwhile, went straight to an armchair and ordered tea. "Oh darling, no …" she'd say, occasionally. "No, please don't do that."

At six minutes to midnight, the airport manager arrived. He asked the family either to control itself or leave. Mother looked aghast. "Is there a problem?" she asked. "What have we done?"

"Madam, look at the mess! Never in my life have I seen such … destruction!"

Joe hated doing it, but he'd studied the instructions. He picked up his half-eaten burger and threw it hard at the manager's back.

"Strrr … rike!" he yelled, as the food exploded over the man's suit. Sure enough, that was the incident that triggered their noisy expulsion from the lounge. Percival was shouting, their mother was crying, and Joe fought with the man holding his T-shirt.

Tilly, however, had moved in the other direction. Unnoticed because of the commotion, she unzipped her rabbit and took out her cellpad. Holding it against an "Authorized Personnel Door – Strictly No Admittance", she obtained its code, and innocently pushed the buttons to open it. With her backpack and rabbit back between her shoulders, she looked like any other curious toddler determined to explore.

The passage led to a hatch that looked over a private runway. Tilly saw a large car cruise carefully through the jumble of baggage vehicles, towards a dark aeroplane. The villains were clearly on time. A conveyor belt, labelled FREIGHT LOADER 20 had been rolled to its cargo-hatch, ready for luggage. It was now exactly midnight, and Tilly alerted Lizards Five and Seven.

Two gentlemen in boiler suits jumped out of the vehicle, the first with a laptop case chained to his wrist. They took two red suitcases from the back seat and put them onto the belt. It was a simple job to turn on the belt and the cases started off on their journey.

Tilly moved quickly. In a second she had her
rabbit in her hands, and, switching the pad's
electronics to a high-frequency scramble-mode,
she activated a stream of data that brought the
belt to a standstill. The precious cargo was left
high and dry above the owners' heads.

"I don't believe it … " said the first man. It was at that point – midnight-zero-one – that Percival, back in the terminal, stared around.

"Hey, Mum. Have we lost Tilly? I don't see her anymore."

"Oh no!" said Joe. "We've lost Tilly! Tilly's back there somewhere!"

The children's mother froze and her face went white. They only had a few seconds to create the diversion that would allow them to support Lizard Three.

"What are you saying to me?" said Mother.

"We've lost our baby sister!" cried Percival. "She's back there!"

"Tilly's gone?"

"She's done a runner! That's what we're saying!"

A small crowd was gathering. In her anxiety and shock, Mother dropped two bottles of duty-free perfume, which smashed and foamed all over the concourse. She turned, slipped in the foam, and fell heavily onto her backside.

"Oh Tilly!" she wailed. "Don't just stand there, Humphrey!"

It took Joe a moment to remember she
was referring to him. "All right, I'll get her!"
he sighed. Hands in pockets, he stomped
back through the lounge with Percival close
behind him.

A tall cleaner was moving quickly towards
them with a mop, keen to assist. "Can I help
you, young man?" he said. He wore a heavy
beard and frizzy hair, but Joe recognized him at
once as their pilot, Ringo.

Meanwhile, at the freight loader, the red suitcases remained stranded. The two villains were staring up at them, unable to believe their bad luck.

The man with the laptop fiddled with the control panel, while his companion moved to the foot of the belt. He was clearly wondering whether or not to start climbing when a tiny girl appeared in front of him and tottered happily onto the machine. Singing as she went, she ascended the conveyor belt, and was soon pushing at the first case. It was midnight-zero-three. The man watched in horror.

Tilly looked at him and smiled. Then, with both hands, she pushed the case over the edge. Both men screamed and ran towards it, but Joe was there first. He caught it with both hands and threw it to Ringo, who'd just arrived. Tilly threw the second case to Percival.

At once, the men were reaching for their weapons, but Joe was already cartwheeling towards the one with the laptop.

His legs found the man's waist and brought him heavily to the ground, crushing the breath from his lungs. Joe swiftly linked the man's ankles so he couldn't move, and reached out for the laptop case.

It took less than five seconds to use his cellpad's grinding-blade to cut through the chain.

Ringo was off at a run with the cases. The second villain managed only to aim before he fell stunned against the belt. Tilly had jumped down onto his back and had her cellpad pressed to his neck.

It was a simple matter then to cable-tie wrists and feet, and to restart the belt. In seconds both men were rising into the cargo hold of their own plane. Ringo reappeared, this time at the controls of his aircraft. The tyres skidded as he swerved towards the Lizards, and they threw themselves through the open door. The precious laptop bounced down the aisle.

Then it was a terrifying taxi out to the runway, where – as an airliner began its ear-shattering take-off – Ringo threw the little plane right behind it. They were airborne in its slipstream, zipping low over the city towards the border.

Chapter 5

They landed just before eight o'clock in the morning, UK time. Joe dragged his school uniform back on, and was driven straight out through the security gates. He was just in time to hear the bell for school assembly. He sprinted down the corridor to catch up with his class. Breathless and sweating, he stepped into line, only to feel a hand on his shoulder.

"Cutting it fine, aren't we, McGinty?"

"Yes, sir," gasped Joe. "I'm sorry, I was … " He noticed his classmates staring at him. "I was ill yesterday, sir. Nasty illness."

"Yes, we noted your absence." The headmaster looked at him with dislike. "I told you you'd get no privileges here, boy. Look at the state of you! Is this how you normally dress? How dare you?"

"Oh … "

"I won't have sloppiness, McGinty! Get to my office now!"

Joe sat and tried to straighten his bird's nest of hair. His adrenalin was still pumping but he was just a schoolboy again!

He re-tied his tie. In the distance he could hear the morning hymn being sung, but his mind was still in the clouds. He tucked in his shirt, and then – checking he was unobserved – slipped out his cellpad. It had a calendar and he studied the display. Every Thursday glowed red on the screen. The next one was four agonizingly long, tedious school-days away, and he wasn't sure he could endure them.

A message flashed up, and he heard a soft, metallic voice: "Bravo, Lizard Seven. Success. See. You. Next … Week."

Then a single word flashed up, white on black, and disappeared: Zeus.

Sharks

Chapter
1

Joe McGinty, otherwise known as Lizard Seven, was in the throbbing hull of a nuclear submarine. Next to him sat Percival, Lizard Five.

"Do you know where we're going, Five?" said Joe.

"Not yet, Seven, no."

"How fast does a submarine actually go?"

"Well this one's nuclear, so anything up to forty knots. We could be anywhere."

Joe scrolled through some information in his own cellpad, and paused at a diagram of an aqualung.

"Looks like we're going to be diving. Have you dived before?"

"Once."

"Looks fairly straightforward … "

Both boys were wearing wetsuits. They looked particularly uncomfortable as they'd been hauled on over lumpy school blazers.

Joe had been taken to Brighton by his gran, and the sub had been waiting just beyond the end of the pier. In the cold light of dawn, a dinghy had floated them out to it. Ringo steered, disguised as a lifeguard.

"Ready for trouble?" he'd said. "This one's more dangerous."

In the submarine, Joe sat back and scrolled though his cellpad. It was an ingenious gadget and communication was just one of its functions.

Its toolbox had an assortment of practical devices such as cutters, winches and even an electric stun facility. The instruction booklet was 6 centimetres thick, and Joe was still only halfway through.

"We're behind schedule, you know," said an impatient voice. A tall, slender girl had appeared in the doorway. Her hair was a snake's nest of intricate braids. "I'm Lizard Four. Salome for this mission, and I've got the meat and the shark-repellent. The pedalo's easy, so I suggest Five takes the controls once we're clear."

"Pedalo?" said Joe.

"Yes."

"I'm afraid I haven't read the whole brief yet. The headmaster wouldn't let me miss assembly, so – "

"Well you should have got up earlier," snapped Salome. "That's boys for you, I suppose – wasting time and finding excuses. Now I'm lead Lizard, so you're following me – and we're running late already. You've read the evening papers, I presume? We're moving in on a syndicate of international pirates, who've taken a child: Davy Tiger-Hampton. His father's Lord Tiger-Hampton, one of the richest businessmen in the UK and a personal friend of the Prime Minister. Davy's quite a handful, it seems. It's all very embarrassing, except it won't be – because we're going to get him back. We'll put an end to the scandal before it starts."

"Right," said Lizard Five.

"I haven't read the papers," said Joe, apologetically. "I had so much homework – "

Salome sighed. "It was Davy's sixth birthday party on the PM's private yacht. He was abducted during a game of hide-and-seek and the pirates' speedboat outpaced every security vessel. Our mission is to find-and-restore. We infiltrate as a trio of lost children. Now according to my cellpad, we're close to the connection zone. We should be disembarking."

Joe and Percival stood up.

"Let's get up to B-deck," said Salome. "The cover's simple – we were on a school trip, studying lighthouses. We left the main group and hired the pedalo, pedalling out to sea like a bunch of idiots. We got swept away by the current so are now in a state of trauma, praying for rescue. Lizard Seven, you drown at 16:25 – "

"You want me to drown?" said Joe.

"You fake it, you fool – read your brief. Any more questions?"

Joe didn't dare.

"Now, turn to channel 909," said Salome. "That's the boy we're rescuing."

An image of a plump-faced child with ratty eyes floated onto the screens of their cellpads. He blinked bad-temperedly and started to grizzle. He appeared to be banging his fists on the table.

"David Tiger-Hampton," ran the caption. "Kidnap danger-level: red. Ransom currently set at twelve million pounds, rising hourly. Child will walk plank at midnight into shark-infested waters."

"Are there really sharks?" whispered Joe to Percival.

"Definitely," said Salome. "The area's totally infested, so don't provoke them. Get your gear on."

A few moments later they had all donned masks, flippers and aqualungs and were in the exit chamber. Salome spun the wheel of the hatch, and put her thumbs up.

The Lizards shot off into the water together.

Chapter 2

Joe was surprised at the warmth of the sea.

He kicked with his flippers and adjusted the oxygen supply. With Salome speeding ahead of him there wasn't time to panic, and the submarine plunged away beneath them. Fish spiralled around their heads as they rose and the boys broke the surface moments after their leader. A bright yellow pedalo bobbed on the waves, with a parachute trailing from its rear end. It had clearly just been dropped for them.

They climbed aboard and peeled off their wetsuits. All three were wearing the same school uniform. They stowed away their diving equipment, and Salome took a satchel from her waterproof bag. She tipped it over the water and some large pieces of raw meat fell into the water. The chunks of red flesh bobbed disturbingly around the little craft.

"Now don't forget," Salome said. "We're in extreme distress. Seven, you lost your arm at 16:21, which means you go overboard at 16:24. That's when the pirates – "

"Lose my arm?" said Joe.

"Oh, for goodness sake!" said Salome angrily. "Read your brief! We were told you had a photographic memory."

"I do, but I'm not used to the cellpad filing system. Oh … here it is."

Joe scrolled through the pages as Salome grabbed his blazer sleeve. She flipped her own cellpad round to the 'tools' function, and extended a razor-sharp cutting wheel. It took seconds to saw through the stitching, and she then concentrated on shredding the shirt sleeve. She glugged a bottle of blood over her handiwork.

"Look, they're coming up – get ready!"

Joe looked into the water. With a lurch of his stomach, he saw that the meat was being nosed by some silvery grey shapes. Salome pushed him, and he sprawled over the side with his bare arm concealed across his chest.

There was a flurry of fins and teeth.

"At least try to look pale," said Salome,
impatiently. "You've lost an arm and masses of
blood."

Joe did his best.

Lizard Five let off three distress flares and
within minutes the bows of a huge powerboat
were alongside them. The vessel swerved
to starboard, sending a wave that nearly
overturned them.

"Oh, my goodness, help!" shrieked Salome.
"He's nearly dead!"

Percival was waving his arms.

"What is your business?" yelled a man
through a megaphone.

"Rescue!" cried Salome. "Thank goodness
you've found us!"

"Keep your hands where we can see them! Identify yourselves!"

"We're just children," sobbed Salome. "We've been drifting for days! My friend's been attacked by sharks – look!"

"Have you got a first-aid kit?" shouted Percival. "He was just leaning over the side … "

"Where are you from?" boomed a voice.

"We're from Green Cross Secondary School," shouted Salome. "Our teachers are going to be furious – please, help us."

Joe had his eyes half closed but he could see the men conferring with each other. They were wearing thick leather jackets, and their faces were hidden by dark glasses and peaked caps. One of them was muttering into a radio.

A lifeline was flung into Salome's hands, and Joe prepared himself for his big performance. He allowed Percival to haul him to his feet, but – at the crucial moment, and with his most theatrical gurgle of pain – he fell backwards into the water. Salome's screams were still ringing in his ears as he let himself drop under the pedalo. He grabbed the aqualung he'd left ready.

The powerboat's propellers were turning very slowly, and as Joe swam towards them, they came to a stop. He had a window of thirty seconds at the most.

He tapped his cellpad, and its power-driver emerged. This was a flat titanium finger that could both turn and grip – the perfect gadget for obstinate screw heads. The tool bit, and Joe felt the strain right up to his shoulders. He was just beginning to think how easy things had been, when a large watery eye came close to his diving-mask. Under it was a zip of irregular teeth. Mercifully, the 'blood' Salome had used on his shoulder was a shark-repellent jelly, so after a little half-hearted sniffing, the creature swam away.

Joe breathed a sigh of relief.

The propeller slipped off its shaft and fell deep into the water below. The boy hauled himself through the narrow opening and found himself in the engine housing. Pressing the cellpad again, he selected a diamond-tipped grinding disc and was soon through the hull. Then he let the navigation system guide him under the machinery and up into one of the inspection chambers. He tapped in his code for Salome: "Craft disabled. In position, and coming up."

Chapter
3

Salome and Percival, meanwhile, were doing their best to appear weak and traumatised. They shivered and wept, while the bemused crew talked over them.

"Put them in the captain's cabin," said the man in charge. "Seems to me we've got three idiots now, instead of one."

"We won't get much money for these two, sir."

"They'll come in useful. They might keep the brat quiet."

At that moment, a high-pitched whine echoed up a nearby stairwell. "I want more pizza! What's going on? Where have my presents gone?"

"Can't we gag him, sir?" said one of the men.

"He's too valuable. Get him more food."

"We don't have any more pizza – "

"Ice cream, then!"

"He finished it!"

The first pirate looked at Salome. "Keep the brat occupied, before there's a mutiny."

In a short time, the two Lizards were ushered down to a small cabin. There, sprawled angrily on the bed, was Davy Tiger-Hampton, his mouth smeared in chocolate. He was surrounded by sweet wrappers, cartons and cans, and was banging a TV remote against the wall.

"I want cartoons," he wailed. "Bring me more sweets!"

Salome stared at the child coldly. The door closed behind them and there was the sound of a key turning.

"Davy," said Salome. "Listen carefully – "

"What?" he said, rudely. "Why should I?"

"You've got to be a good boy," said Percival. "You've got to do exactly as you're told."

"Says who?" said Davy. "My daddy's rich and if he – "

"Oh, do be quiet!" said Salome, losing patience. "We're here to save you, you idiot, so stand up and put this on."

"No, I won't! Wait till my daddy hears – "

His words were muffled as Salome slipped a diving mask over the child's podgy face. Suddenly, he stopped struggling and stared.

The wardrobe door had opened, and the soaking-wet figure of Joe appeared, aqualung dangling from his shoulders.

"Message from Ringo," he gasped. "Three minutes to pick-up."

Davy pulled off the mask. "I want my sweets," he screamed. "This is my party and you're spoiling it!" A major tantrum was clearly brewing.

"Strategy Two?" said Salome.

"Definitely," said Percival.

They worked together, and in a moment they had trussed the child's arms and legs with elastic straps and drawn a waterproof bag up to his chin. As his mouth opened to scream, they popped the oxygen mouthpiece into it, and fixed a small oxygen tank onto his back.

Salome picked up the writhing child and slung him over her shoulder. She was stronger than she looked.

They followed the tunnel Joe had cut, back through the wardrobe to the boat's tiny engine room. It was already half underwater. They plunged down, groping their way through the hole Joe had torn open, and swam out of the hull.

The Lizards paused, taking turns to gulp oxygen from Joe's aqualung. Before they could get their bearings, however, two pirates had appeared. They had been inspecting the broken propeller, but saw at once that their hostage was escaping. They went straight for their weapons.

In a flash, Salome shot forward and there was an explosion of bubbles. She cut through the pirates' breathing apparatus and, turning behind them, kicked with both feet. The two men were sent spinning upwards. As they flapped helplessly, a truly monstrous shark raced into view. It came between the two men like a missile, knocking them sideways. The mouth opened, and the Lizards saw two racks of needle-sharp teeth. Demonic eyes stared straight at them and the mouth got wider and wider.

There was nowhere to hide, and the monster was on them in a moment, sucking them down. Joe found himself swirling through the shark's throat in a tangle of arms and legs. Then he was dropping into its belly.

It widened out, and Joe noticed straps and a wooden floor. There were four wooden seats, and he realised he was safely in the rescue vessel.

Beside the four children, on a raised platform, was Ringo. He was peering through the shark's eyeballs, and a firm hand eased the throttle open. Soon, the vessel was speeding through the deep, its tail flapping.

"Mission accomplished?" he said, winking at Joe. "There are towels above your seats."

The three children sat back, catching their breath. Beside them, Davy Tiger-Hampton wriggled, his mouth still clamped around the breathing apparatus. They decided not to remove it, even when they docked with the submarine fifteen minutes later.

Chapter 4

The next morning, Joe ran like the wind.

The taxi had dropped him just outside the school gates, but it was five past nine and the first lesson had already started. He was aware of a strong whiff of the sea about him, but he tugged his fingers through his hair and hoped no one would notice. He was ready for the school day if only he could slip in unnoticed. Using one of the school's back doors, he thought he'd been successful when a voice echoed down the corridor.

"McGinty! Stop!"

McGinty! Stop!

Joe turned.

The headmaster was red with fury.

"What is the meaning of this? Is this fancy dress? What on earth are you playing at?"

He leaned over Joe, and hissed in his ear.

"When I gave permission for these weekly absences, it was on the strict condition you'd be presentable the following day. Now get to my office!"

Joe found himself sitting by the door, his ruined blazer on his knees. He had forgotten about the shredded sleeve, and his shirt was still covered in fake blood. Once again his appearance had let him down.

Joe sighed, then – carefully – took out his cellpad. Just like last time, the calendar showed every Thursday in glowing red. Each one winked at him mischievously. He had another four days of school to endure before the next mission.

A message flashed up and he heard the same metallic voice that he'd heard last time: "Bravo, Lizard Seven. Excellent work. See. You. Next … Week. For the big one."

Then the single word floated to the surface, white on black: